CAN YOU COUNT TEN TOES?

Count to 10 in 10 Different Languages

Lezlie Evans *Illustrated by* **Denis Roche**

Houghton Mifflin Company
Boston 1999

Can you count ten toes, ten toes?
Count them if you please.
Count the toes from one to ten,
but count in **Japanese.**

① **いち** ichi (ee-chee)

② **に** ni (nee)

③ **さん** san (sahn)

④ **し** shi (she)

⑤ **ご** go (go)

⑥ **ろく** roku (roe-koo)

⑦ **しち** shichi (she-chee)

⑧ **はち** hachi (ha-chee)

⑨ **きゅう** ku (koo)

⑩ **じゅう** ju (joo)

Can you count the orbs in space,
nine planets plus the sun?
Try to speak in **Russian** as
you count them one by one.

① ОДИН odin (ah-DEEN)

② ДВА dva (dvah)

③ ТРИ tri (tree)

④ ЧЕТЫРЕ chetyre (chih-TIR-ee)

⑤ ПЯТЬ pyat (pyat)

⑥ ШЕСТЬ shest (shayst)

⑦ СЕМЬ sem (syem)

⑧ ВОСЕМЬ vosem (VOH-syem)

⑨ ДЕВЯТЬ devyat (DYEH-vit)

⑩ ДЕСЯТЬ desyat (DYEH-sit)

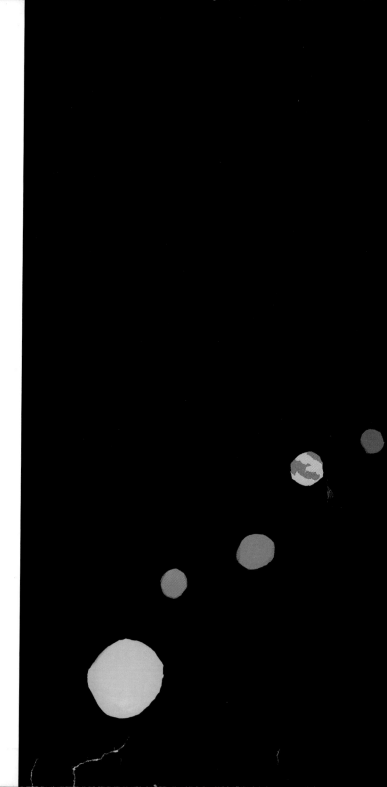

Can you count the angelfish swimming in the sea? You can speak **Korean** as you count them, one, two, three.

① **하나** hana (HA-nah)

② **둘** tul (tool)

③ **셋** set (set)

④ **넷** net (net)

⑤ **다섯** tasot (TAH-sut)

⑥ **여섯** yosot (YUH-sut)

⑦ **일곱** ilgop (ILL-gup)

⑧ **여덟** yodol (YUH-dul)

⑨ **아홉** ahup (AH-hope)

⑩ **열** yol (yul)

Can you count the different coins
spread across the table?
Speaking now in **Zulu,** try to
count them, if you're able.

1 **kunye (koo-NYAH)**

2 **kubili (koo-BEE-lee)**

3 **kuthathu (koo-TAH-too)**

4 **kune (koo-NEH)**

5 **kuhlanu (koo-THA-noo)**

6 **isithupha (ee-see-TOO-pa)**

7 **isikhombisa (ee-see-kom-BEE-sa)**

8 **shiyagalombili (she-ya-ka-lom-BEE-lee)**

9 **shiyagalolunye (she-ya-ka-lon-LOON-yeh)**

10 **shiumi (SHOE-me)**

Can you count the ten balloons
floating in the sky?
Count each one, but count in **French**
before they pass you by!

① **un** (uhn)

② **deux** (duh)

③ **trois** (twah)

④ **quatre** (kat)

⑤ **cinq** (sank)

⑥ **six** (seece)

⑦ **sept** (set)

⑧ **huit** (weet)

⑨ **neuf** (nuhf)

⑩ **dix** (deece)

Can you count the different hats
hanging on the wall?
As you count in **Hindi,** please
be sure to count them all.

1 १ **ek** (ache)

2 २ **do** (doe)

3 ३ **tin** (teen)

4 ४ **char** (char)

5 ५ **panch** (ponch)

6 ६ **chha** (chay)

7 ७ **sat** (sot)

8 ८ **ath** (ahrt)

9 ९ **nau** (now)

10 १० **das** (duss)

Count the children on the bus,
count them, one, two, three.
Speak now in **Tagalog** as
you count each child you see.

① **isa** (ee-SAH)

② **dalawa** (dah-lah-WAH)

③ **tatlo** (taht-LOH)

④ **apat** (AH-paht)

⑤ **lima** (lee-MAH)

⑥ **anim** (AH-neem)

⑦ **pito** (pee-TOH)

⑧ **walo** (wah-LOH)

⑨ **siyam** (see-YAHM)

⑩ **sampu** (sahm-POH)

Can you count ten different boats
floating in the bay?
Count each one in **Hebrew** now
before they sail away.

① אחת **achat** (ah-KHOT)

② שתיים **shtayim** (SHTY-eem)

③ שלוש **shalosh** (sha-LOSH)

④ ארבע **arba** (ar-BAH)

⑤ חמש **chamesh** (khah-MAYSH)

⑥ שש **shesh** (shaysh)

⑦ שבע **sheva** (sheh-VAH)

⑧ שמונה **shmone** (shmo-NEH)

⑨ תשע **tesha** (TAY-shah)

⑩ עשר **eser** (ES-sair)

Can you count the lightning bugs?
Quick, before they vanish!
Count each bug from one to ten,
saying it in **Spanish.**

❶ uno (OO-no)

❷ dos (dose)

❸ tres (trace)

❹ cuatro (KWA-tro)

❺ cinco (SING-ko)

❻ seis (sace)

❼ siete (see-EH-tay)

❽ ocho (O-cho)

❾ nueve (NWEH-vay)

❿ diez (DEE-es)

Can you count each country's flag
waving in the breeze?
Try to count them one by one,
but count them in **Chinese.**

① 一 **yi** (ee)

② 二 **er** (are)

③ 三 **san** (sahn)

④ 四 **si** (suh)

⑤ 五 **wu** (woo)

⑥ 六 **liu** (leo)

⑦ 七 **qi** (chee)

⑧ 八 **ba** (bah)

⑨ 九 **jiu** (jeo)

⑩ 十 **shi** (shr)

Now you've counted one through ten
in many different tongues,
but no matter how you say it
counting can be fun!

Can you count each colored dot?
Count them one by one.
Spot them all and you will learn
where they speak each tongue.

Chinese (Mandarin)
1. China
2. Taiwan
3. Singapore

Hindi
4. India

Hebrew
5. Israel

Japanese
6. Japan

Tagalog
7. Philippines

Russian
8. Russia

Zulu
9. South Africa

Korean
10. North Korea
11. South Korea

Spanish
12. Spain
13. Mexico
14. Colombia
15. Argentina
16. Chile
17. Cuba
18. Dominican Republic
19. Equatorial Guinea
20. Ecuador
21. Venezuela
22. Costa Rica
23. Nicaragua
24. Honduras
25. Guatemala
26. Panama
27. El Salvador
28. Peru
29. Bolivia
30. Paraguay
31. Uruguay

French
32. France
33. Belgium
34. Switzerland
35. Canada
36. Haiti
37. Monaco
38. Benin
39. Burkina Faso
40. Burundi
41. Cameroon
42. Central African Republic
43. Chad
44. Republic of the Congo
45. Côte d'Ivoire
46. Djibouti
47. Gabon
48. Guinea
49. Luxembourg
50. Madagascar
51. Mauritania
52. Niger
53. Rwanda
54. Senegal
55. Seychelles
56. Togo
57. Democratic Republic
of the Congo

Here are some of the countries in which these languages are officially spoken.